This edition published 2009, by Zero to Ten Limited,
part of the Evans Publishing Group
2A Portman Mansions
Chiltern St
London W1U 6NR

British Library Cataloguing in Publication Data
A CIP catalogue record for this book Is available from the British
Library

ISBN: 9781840895711

Printed in Hong Kong by New Era Co. Ltd

Fred
and
Finn

by Madeline Goodey

illustrated by Mike Gordon

ZERO TO TEN

Fat frog Finn and
thin frog Fred
were jumping up
and down.

Along came a fly.

Up jumped fat Finn and grabbed that tasty fly!

Thin Fred was too slow.

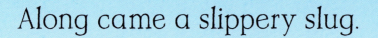

Along came a slippery slug.

Down jumped fat Finn and ...

... gobbled up that slippery slug.

Thin frog Fred was too slow,
again.

Along came a
lovely bug.

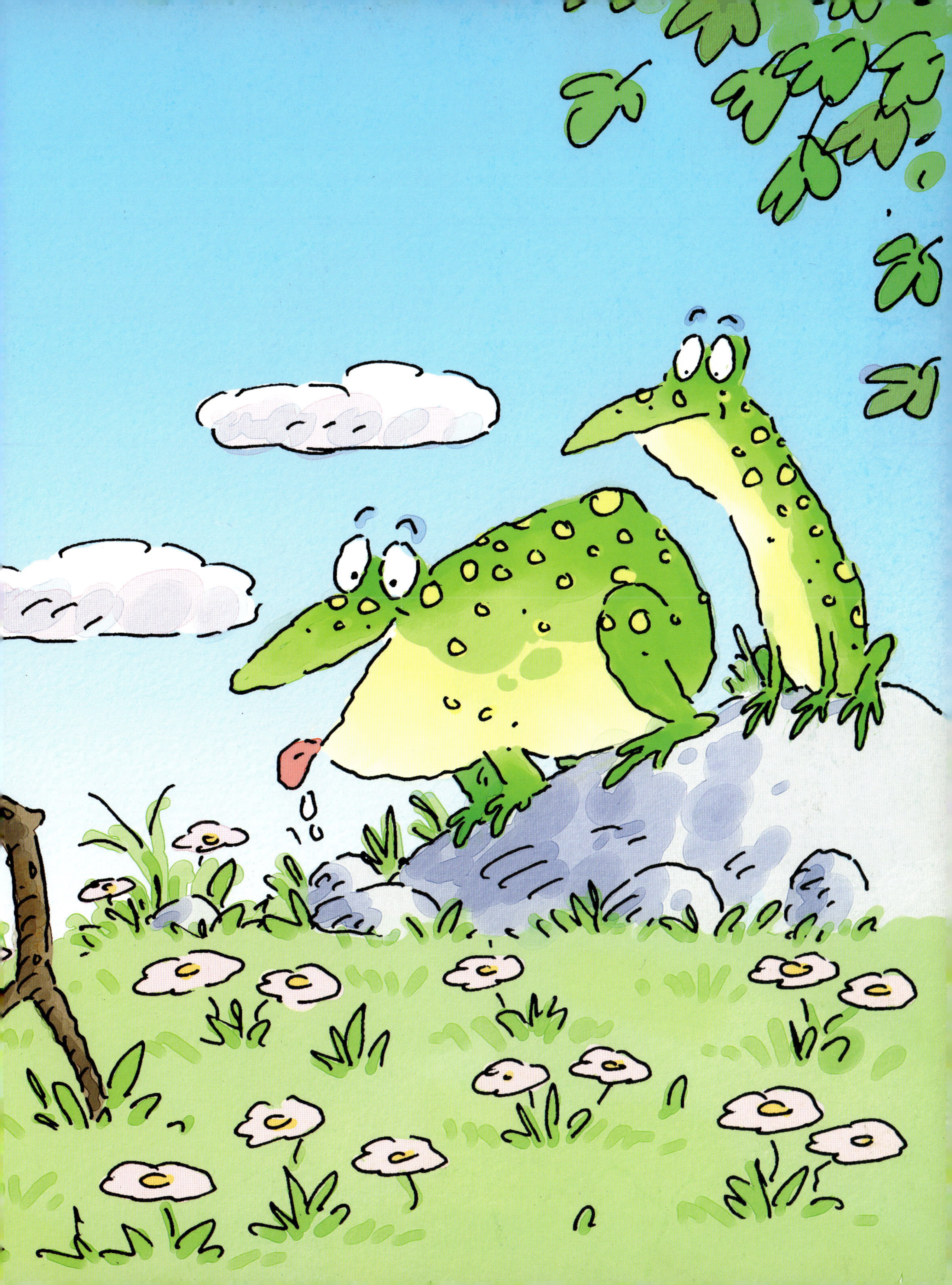

Under the branch
jumped fat frog Finn ...

... and got stuck!
He couldn't move.

Thin frog Fred jumped over
the branch and ate that
lovely bug. At last!

Fat frog Finn could not move.

Thin frog Fred munched
on a juicy caterpillar.

Fat frog Finn still could
not move.

Thin frog
Fred had a
berry for his
pudding.

So fat frog Finn got thin and
thin frog Fred got fat!